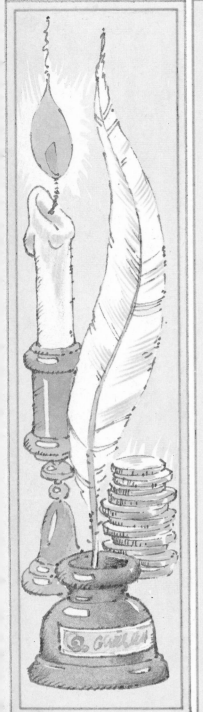

This book belongs to

© 1992 Grandreams Limited.

This edition published in 1995.

A Christmas Carol, The Little Fir Tree & The Nutcracker re-told
by Anne McKie.

Illustrated by Ken McKie.

Published by
GRANDREAMS LIMITED
Jadwin House, 205/211 Kentish Town Road, London, NW5 2JU.

Printed in Czech Republic.

XM7

A Treasury of
WELL LOVED
CHRISTMAS
TALES

A Christmas Carol
The Night Before Christmas
The Little Fir Tree
The Nutcracker

This classic Christmas story written
by Charles Dickens, takes place in London
during the reign of Queen Victoria.
Ebenezer Scrooge is known to everyone
as a mean and unkind man.
Then late one Christmas Eve, the ghost of
his old partner Jacob Marley appears
and warns him that he must change his ways...

Ebenezer
Scrooge

Tiny Tim
Cratchit

Bob Cratchit

The Ghost of
Jacob Marley

The Spirit of
Christmas Past

The Spirit of
Christmas Present

The Spirit of
Christmas
To Come

A CHRISTMAS CAROL

Re-told by Anne McKie.
Illustrated by Ken McKie.

Once upon a time - on Christmas Eve - Ebenezer Scrooge sat busy in his counting-house.

A faded sign hung above his office door that read: "Scrooge and Marley". Jacob Marley had been Scrooge's business partner, but he had died over seven years ago, and Scrooge was such an old skinflint he wouldn't pay for a new sign to be put up.

It was cold, bleak, biting weather that day and the thick fog outside came pouring in through every chink and keyhole. But Scrooge never felt the winter chill, for he was a mean, tight-fisted old miser with a heart as cold as ice. He never did a kind deed or helped anyone, although he had piles of money locked away . . . and most of all he hated CHRISTMAS!

All day long Scrooge left his office door wide open to keep his eye on his clerk, Bob Cratchit, even on Christmas Eve. The poor fellow was so cold he had to work in his coat and scarf. And the fire Scrooge allowed him to have was so small it looked like one coal.

"A Merry Christmas, Uncle!" cried a cheerful voice. It was Scrooge's nephew, Fred, who had called to wish him the very best for the festive season.

"Bah!" cried Scrooge. "Humbug!"

"Don't be angry, Uncle. Come and share Christmas dinner with us tomorrow," said his nephew kindly.

The very word CHRISTMAS made Scrooge angry. "If I had my way," shouted Scrooge, "every idiot who goes around wishing people 'Merry Christmas', should be boiled with his own Christmas pudding and buried with a stake of holly through his heart. Keep Christmas in your own way and let me keep it in mine!" And Scrooge pointed to the door.

As he left, Fred stopped to wish Bob Cratchit a 'Merry Christmas'. The poor man was trying to warm his freezing hands by a candle flame.

The afternoon got foggier and darker and colder. A little boy bent down to sing a carol at Scrooge's keyhole, but at the first few notes of:

"God rest you, merry gentlemen,
May nothing you dismay!"

Scrooge grabbed his ruler and the poor boy fled in terror.

At last the time came to stop work and close the office. Bob Cratchit blew out his candle and put on his hat.

"I suppose you want all day off tomorrow," snapped Scrooge.

"If that's alright, sir," said Bob Cratchit timidly. "It's only once a year, and it is Christmas Day!"

"It is not alright!" replied Scrooge. "Just remember that I will have to pay you a whole day's wage for no work!" and Scrooge left with a growl.

Bob Cratchit locked up the office in a twinkling. On the way home - just because it was Christmas - he went down an icy slide twenty times, just for the fun of it!

Scrooge, on the other hand, ate his supper all alone at a nearby inn, and went home to bed.

He lived by himself in a dark old house that had once belonged to his partner, Jacob Marley.

Now, that Christmas Eve, as Scrooge put his key in the lock, he looked up, and instead of the brass door-knocker, he saw Marley's face!

As Scrooge stared in amazement, it turned into a door-knocker again.

At once Scrooge unlocked his door, and hurried inside and quickly lit a candle. Then he took a good look around all the rooms, just to make sure no-one was there. He even looked under the bed!

Quite satisfied, he locked his bedroom door and put on his dressing gown, his slippers and nightcap.

All of a sudden, an old bell that hung by the fireplace began to swing to and fro. Soon it began to ring out loudly - and so did every bell in the house.

Then Scrooge heard a different sound, as if someone was dragging heavy chains from the cellar, up the stairs and into his bedroom.

Poor Scrooge's knees began to knock and his teeth began to chatter as JACOB MARLEY'S GHOST floated through the door!

At first Scrooge thought his eyes were playing tricks, or his supper had given him indigestion. But the ghost did look like his old friend Jacob Marley, although it was covered from head to foot in chains, and loaded down with heavy cash-boxes, bunches of keys and big metal padlocks.

"I have come to warn you, Ebenezer Scrooge," wailed the ghost, "before it's too late!" And he rattled his chains at Scrooge.

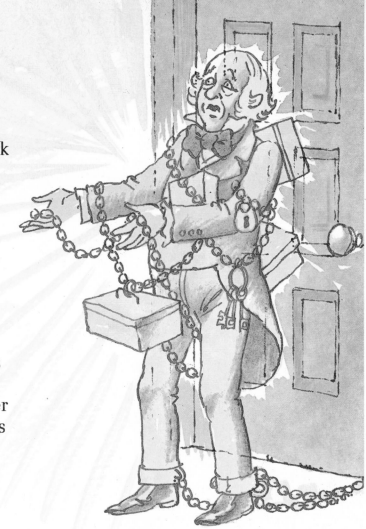

"If you do not mend your ways at once, and become kind, loving and give to other people, you will end up like me!" the ghost went on. "In my life I cared for nothing but money. And look at me now. A lonely old ghost, deemed to wander around with nothing but money-boxes for company!"

Scrooge shuddered. "Tell me, dear friend, how can I change?"

By now the ghost was floating towards the window, his voice fading. "You will be visited by three Spirits when the clock strikes one. Listen to them, Ebenezer Scrooge, and you will escape my fate!"

And with that, the ghost of Jacob Marley floated out into the dark night and vanished among the chimney pots.

Feeling very tired, Scrooge closed the window, crept into bed and fell fast asleep.

A nearby clock struck midnight and Scrooge woke up. Feeling very nervous he lay awake until one. Would he see the first of the three Spirits - or had it all been a bad dream?

On the stroke of one, light filled the room. The curtains of his bed were drawn back and Scrooge found himself face to face with a ghost! It was a very strange ghost, small like a child, with long white hair.

"Who or what are you?" asked Scrooge.

"I am the Ghost of Christmas Past," said the Spirit in a gentle voice. "I am here to remind you of your past!"

The Spirit whisked Scrooge, still in his dressing gown and slippers, up in the air and out into the dark night . . . and back in time!

The city had vanished and they found themselves in a little country town. Scrooge was a boy again surrounded by his school friends.

All the boys were going home for the Christmas holidays. Sad to say, no-one came to fetch young Ebenezer that year. So he was left alone at school to spend a miserable Christmas all by himself.

When Scrooge remembered this he began to cry. The Spirit smiled and waved his hand. "Let us see another Christmas!"

Scrooge saw himself sitting in the schoolroom a few years later. Again all his friends had gone home for the Christmas holiday.

Suddenly, the door opened and his beloved sister, Fran, darted in. She flung her arms round his neck and kissed him.

"I have come to bring you home! Not just for the holidays, but for ever and ever!"

Quick as a flash, the Spirit whisked Scrooge away from his old school. In no time at all they were outside a warehouse door and the Spirit asked Scrooge if he knew the place.

"Know it! I was an apprentice there!" cried Scrooge excitedly.

They went in. Scrooge could see himself as a young gentleman, having a marvellous time at the office Christmas party.

His old boss, Mr. Fezziwig, had ordered all his young apprentices to stop work and join the family in fun and games. There was music and dancing and presents for all.

Poor Scrooge remembered how happy he had been in those days, but now he cared more about money than friends. And he had forgotten how to have fun.

The Spirit of Christmas Past had made Scrooge see what a lonely miserable old man he had become.

Suddenly Scrooge realised that he was back in his own bedroom. Tired out, he fell fast asleep.

All too soon he was awakened in the middle of a huge snore by a clock striking one.

As he peered over the bedclothes, Scrooge saw the whole place filled with rosy light from the next room.

Trembling, he got up and shuffled in his slippers to the door.

"Come in! Come in!" boomed a voice. "I am the Spirit of Christmas Present! Come in and get to know me!"

Scrooge entered timidly, and what a sight met his eyes. The room was full to bursting with Christmas fayre. And right in the middle sat a cheery fat giant of a ghost.

"Touch my robe!" said the Spirit of Christmas Present.

Scrooge did as he was told and held on tight.

Everything in the room vanished and Scrooge found himself walking through the cold snowy city streets together with the Spirit.

It was Christmas morning and the shops were still open. The grocer's, the baker's, the poulterer's and the fruit shops. All selling Christmas food right up to the very last minute.

Church bells rang out all over the city, calling folks to church. The streets were full of happy bustling people. Some going to worship, while others were carrying their Christmas goose to the baker's - to be cooked in his huge ovens; everyone looking forward to their Christmas dinner.

Quickly the Spirit moved on with Scrooge still hanging tight on to his robe. At last they stopped and slipped, quite unseen, into the home of Scrooge's clerk, Bob Cratchit.

Now this poor fellow had to bring up his family on fifteen shillings a week, for that was all that mean old Scrooge would pay him.

But today it was Christmas Day, and Mrs Cratchit had managed to save enough to make a Christmas dinner - a special dinner that all the Cratchits would remember until next Christmas.

As Scrooge and the Spirit gazed at the happy scene, Mrs Cratchit was busy laying the table for dinner helped by her daughters, while a couple of the younger Cratchits danced round the room getting very excited.

Young Peter was in charge of a great pan of potatoes, bubbling away on the fire. Everybody was simply longing for dinner time.

"Here's Father coming home," cried the two little Cratchits, as Bob came home from church with his son, Tiny Tim, on his shoulder.

Young Tiny Tim was very frail. He had to use a little crutch, and could only walk with an iron frame strapped onto his leg. When he was tired he sat by the fire on his own small stool.

In rushed the young Cratchits carrying the goose that had been roasting in the baker's oven. It was dinner time at last!

The dishes were put on the table and grace was said. Everyone took a deep breath as Mrs Cratchit plunged her carving knife into the hot roast goose, stuffed with sage and onion and served with apple sauce and mashed potatoes. It was enough for the whole family.

Great excitement now as Mrs Cratchit left the room.

She returned, quite flushed, with a Christmas pudding. And what a pudding! It was speckled like a cannonball, blazing with brandy and a sprig of holly on top.

At last dinner was finished, and the whole family sat round the fire with roast chestnuts and some punch. Bob raised his glass. "A Merry Christmas to us all, my dears. God bless us!"

"God bless us everyone!" said Tiny Tim, and Bob reached out and held his frail little hand.

"Spirit," said Scrooge, "tell me if Tiny Tim will live!"

"I see an empty chair," replied the Spirit; "and a crutch without an owner. If things do not change, Tiny Tim will die!"

"No, no," said Scrooge. "Kind Spirit, say he will not die!"

Scrooge hung his head as he remembered how little money he paid Bob Cratchit. It was because of him Bob's family were so poor, so shabby and so often cold and hungry.

That night the Spirit of Christmas Present showed Scrooge many things. They visited places that made Scrooge shudder. They flew over bleak dark moors where miners worked underground. They flew over the raging sea and heard sailors singing carols as they steered the ship through a storm.

Worst of all they saw ragged hungry children with no-one to care for them, even at Christmas. It was then Scrooge remembered that he had never tried to help them, although he had been given many chances.

It had seemed such a long night and the Spirit and Scrooge had travelled far. A bell struck twelve and the Spirit vanished.

As Scrooge looked again, he saw a dark figure drifting towards him through the mist.

"Are you the Spirit of the Future?" whispered Scrooge.

The Spirit did not answer, just pointed. He showed Scrooge people talking about a certain old miser who had just died. No-one was sad, no-one went to his funeral, and no-one missed him or loved him.

Then, without a word, the Spirit of the Future took Scrooge to the home of Bob Cratchit. There he saw the sad faces of the young Cratchits, the empty stool by the fireside and the crutch in the corner. Scrooge realised that Tiny Tim must have died.

"Tell me about my future, Spirit!" begged Scrooge trembling, but the Spirit didn't reply. Instead he led him to a churchyard and pointed at a gravestone.

Scrooge crept towards it and written on the stone was his own name: EBENEZER SCROOGE.

"That can't be me!" cried Scrooge. "I will change! I promise to keep Christmas in my heart all the year round!"

As poor frightened Scrooge tried to grab the Spirit's arm, the black robe collapsed and changed into a bedpost.

Yes, the bedpost was his own, the bed was his own and the room was his own. Best of all, he was alive with lots of time in front of him to change his ways.

Scrooge jumped out of bed laughing and crying in the same breath. He rushed round the room dancing and singing, so happy, he put on all his clothes inside out and back to front.

Running to the window, he opened it and stuck his head out. "What day is it today?" he called to a boy dressed in his best clothes.

"Why, Christmas Day!" replied the lad.

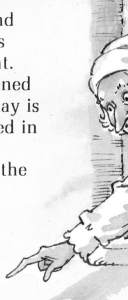

"So, I haven't missed it!" said Scrooge to himself.

Then he told the young boy to run and buy the huge turkey hanging in the poulterer's shop, and he gave the boy half-a-crown for his trouble.

"I'll send it to Bob Cratchit!" chuckled Scrooge. "He'll never guess where it came from. It must be twice as big as Tiny Tim!"

Having paid for the turkey and a man with a cab to take it over to Camden Town, Scrooge felt quite breathless.

No time to waste. Scrooge shaved, then dressed himself up in his best clothes. He went out into the streets calling: "Merry Christmas" to passers by and smiling at everyone he met.

He went to the church and then walked towards his
nephew Fred's house. He passed the door a dozen times
before he plucked up courage to knock.

A girl let him in and Scrooge went straight to the dining
room and poked his head round the door.

"Why bless my soul!" cried his nephew, "who's that?"

"It's your uncle Scrooge. I have come to dinner. Will
you let me in?"

The family gave Scrooge such a warm welcome that he
felt at home in five minutes. He enjoyed a wonderful party
with wonderful games - the old man never felt happier.

Next morning, Scrooge wanted to
be first at the office (just to catch Bob
Cratchit coming in late).

The clock struck nine, no Bob.
Scrooge sat with his door wide open.
At last at eighteen and a half minutes
past nine, Bob arrived.

His hat and scarf were off before he
opened the door. He jumped up on his
stool and began writing away as fast as
he could.

"What do you mean by coming here
at this time of day?" growled Scrooge,
pretending to be angry.

"It's only once a year!" pleaded poor Bob. "I promise it won't happen again!"

"I'm not going to stand this kind of thing any longer!" Scrooge went on, digging Bob Cratchit in the ribs. "And therefore I am about to raise your salary!"

Bob jumped back.

"A Merry Christmas, Bob," said Scrooge slapping him on the back. "A Merrier Christmas than I've given for many a year. Build up the fire; we'll sit together and talk about your wages and how I can help your family!"

Scrooge was better than his word. He did much more than he promised; and to Tiny Tim, who did not die, he was a second father.

Some people laughed at such a change in Scrooge - but he didn't care a bit.

He had no more visits from ghosts or spirits. And it was always said of him that he knew how to keep Christmas as well as any man alive.

May that be said of all of us. As Tiny Tim said: "God Bless Us, Everyone!"

The ghosts who appeared to Ebenezer Scrooge that Christmas Eve showed him what a mean and horrid old man he was.

By being kind and helping others, he became the happy man that he had been when he was younger.

But did the ghosts really come to him, or was it all just a dream?

Ebenezer Scrooge

Tiny Tim Cratchit

Bob Cratchit

The Ghost of
Jacob Marley

The Spirit of
Christmas Past

The Spirit of
Christmas Present

The Spirit of
Christmas
To Come

THE NIGHT BEFORE CHRISTMAS

'Twas the night before Christmas,
   when all through the house
Not a creature was stirring,
   not even a mouse;

The stockings were hung
   by the chimney with care,
In hopes that St. Nicholas
   soon would be there;

The children were nestled
all snug in their beds,
While visions of sugar-plums
danced in their heads;

And Mamma in her kerchief, and I in my cap,
  Had just settled our brains for a long winter's nap;
When out on the lawn there arose such a clatter,
  I sprang from the bed to see what was the matter.

Away to the window I flew like a flash,
  Tore open the shutters, and threw up the sash.
The moon on the breast of the new-fallen snow,
  Gave the lustre of midday to objects below;
When, what to my wondering eyes should appear,
  But a miniature sleigh and eight tiny reindeer,
With a little old driver, so lively and quick,
  I knew in a moment, it must be St. Nick.

More rapid than eagles his coursers they came,
  And he whistled, and shouted, and called them by name:
"Now, Dasher! now, Dancer! now, Prancer and Vixen!
  On, Comet! on, Cupid! on, Donner and Blitzen!

To the top of the porch! to the top of the wall!
    Now dash away! dash away! dash away all!"
As dry leaves that before the wild hurricane fly,
    When they meet with an obstacle, mount to the sky,
So up to the house-top the coursers they flew,
    With the sleigh full of toys, and St. Nicholas too.
And then in a twinkle, I heard on the roof,
    The prancing and pawing, of each little hoof.

As I drew in my head, and was turning around,
    Down the chimney St. Nicholas came with a bound.
He was dressed all in fur, from his head to his foot,
    And his clothes were all tarnished with ashes and soot;
A bundle of toys he flung on his back,
    And he looked like a pedlar just opening his pack.

His eyes - how they twinkled! his dimples how merry!
  His cheeks were like roses, his nose like a cherry!
His droll little mouth was drawn like a bow,
  And the beard on his chin was as white as the snow;
The stump of a pipe he held tight in his teeth,
  And the smoke it encircled his head like a wreath;

He had a broad face and a little round belly,
That shook when he laughed, like a bowlful of jelly.
He was chubby and plump - a right jolly old elf -
And I laughed when I saw him, in spite of myself.
A wink in his eye and a twist of his head,

Soon gave me to know I had nothing to dread.
   He spoke not a word, but went straight to his work,
And filled all the stockings; then turned with a jerk,
   And laying his finger aside of his nose,
And giving a nod, up the chimney he rose;

He sprang to his sleigh,
    to his team gave a whistle,
And away they all flew
    like the down of a thistle.
But I heard him exclaim,
    ere he drove out of sight,
"Happy Christmas to all,
    and to all a good night!"

THE LITTLE FIR TREE

Re-told by Anne McKie. Illustrated by Ken McKie.

Once upon a time, in a clearing deep in the middle of a great forest, there grew a Little Fir Tree.

All around him were giant pine trees with long straight trunks, their top branches almost reaching the sky - well at least, that's how it looked to the Little Fir Tree, who longed to grow tall and tower over the whole forest.

The animals who lived nearby loved the Little Fir Tree. In spring and summer they played all day beneath his soft feathery branches. Small birds built their nests amongst his sweet smelling needles, sheltered from the strong winds that swept through the giant pines high above.

All day long, the Little Fir Tree could hear the sound of axes ringing through the forest, as the woodcutters felled the tallest trees and brought them crashing to the ground.

The Little Fir Tree sighed to himself: "I wish my trunk was tall and straight enough to be a ship's mast, or even the strongest beam in a big house!"

With that, he stretched his small branches as hard as he could, to try and make himself grow a bit bigger.

One day, the wind that swayed the Little Fir Tree's branches began to grow colder and the first few snowflakes of winter started to fall.

The animals all disappeared for their long winter sleep, and most of the birds had flown away to summer lands. Very soon the snow lay thick on the ground - even the woodcutters had left the forest until next spring.

Was the Little Fir Tree lonely? Oh, no! For soon new exciting sounds began to fill the air. It was the laughter and shrieks of happy children, as they tobogganed down the forest's snowy slopes.

All of a sudden the Little Fir Tree was surrounded by three delighted children. They danced around him in the snow, clapping and singing. "We've found the most beautiful tree in the forest," they chorused.

The Little Fir Tree, his branches sparkling and twinkling with frost, almost blushed with pride.

"Father! Come quickly!" all three cried together. "Here is our Christmas Tree!"

Before he knew what was happening, the Little Fir Tree
had been cut down and gently placed on a sledge. Very
soon he was speeding along between the great trunks of
the giant pines, until the forest was left far behind.

Everyone seemed so delighted with the Little Fir Tree
that he felt happy too.

At last they came to the small town at the foot of the forest's slopes.

As the children ran through the streets, they shouted to everybody they met, "Look at our tree! Isn't it the most perfect Christmas Tree you ever saw?"

The Little Fir Tree felt rather puzzled. "What on earth is a Christmas Tree?" he thought to himself.

The Little Fir Tree was beginning to enjoy himself. "This is much better than becoming one of those giant pine trees and living all your life in the forest."

"Where did you get that lovely little tree?" "Is he for sale?" "Please can I buy him?" people shouted as they passed by. The three children just grinned and shook their heads.

All at once, the Little Fir Tree looked around. He saw fir trees everywhere! They were standing in windows, outside front doors, on porches and in gardens.

"These must be Christmas Trees!" smiled the Little Fir Tree, feeling proud. "Then I shall be the very best Christmas Tree of all!"

When the Little Fir Tree reached the children's house,
he was carefully carried inside and placed upright in a tub.
That night, the whole family gathered round to decorate
their Christmas Tree - for it was Christmas Eve.

Everyone helped to hang the decorations on the Little
Fir Tree's branches. Soon this very special little tree was
covered with toys and fruit, cookies and candy, and lots of
tiny candles. And at the very top - a golden star!

There stood the Little Fir Tree quivering with pride. He really was the Most Beautiful Christmas Tree in the World!

The tiny candles twinkled like a thousand stars and filled the room with their sparkling light. The Little Fir Tree shone in all his glory, for it was Christmas Eve - the most magical night of the year.

Before they went to bed on this very special night, the children left their stockings beneath the Little Fir Tree. "No one has ever seen Father Christmas," whispered the children, very excited, "and he won't come until everyone is fast asleep."

But late that night Father Christmas did come. He slipped silently into the room, quietly took the children's presents from his sack and popped them underneath the tree.

Just for a moment he stepped back to admire the beautiful Little Fir Tree. He gave a broad smile, a twinkle of his eye, then vanished up the chimney.

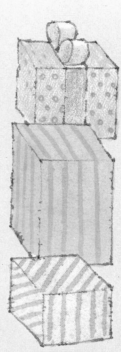

The Little Fir Tree felt so happy to be a Christmas Tree, and very proud that he alone had really seen Father Christmas.

During the twelve days of Christmas, the Little Fir Tree had a wonderful time. Many visitors called at the house to admire him, and lots of children came in from the street to see how beautiful he looked. The Little Fir Tree loved every moment of it, and thought it would last for ever.

All too soon Twelfth Night came, which marked the end of Christmas.

Every single decoration in the house was taken down and packed away until next year.

The Little Fir Tree looked so bare. Lots of his needles
had dropped onto the floor and his branches were brittle
and dry. Worse was to come! Along with all the other old
greenery in the house, the poor Little Fir Tree was taken
outside and burned on the bonfire.

And that was the end of the Little Fir Tree!

The whole family felt sorry that Christmas was over and
that their lovely tree had met such a sad end. So there and
then, the children's father made a promise that it would
not happen again.

During the long cold months of winter that followed,
the family never forgot their Little Fir Tree. The children
remembered his dazzling brilliance, and it made them feel
happy through the dark winter nights.

Spring came at last! The warm sun melted the snow and
ice and the forest came to life once more.

One bright sunny morning, Father took the three
children to the spot where he had cut down the Little Fir
Tree.

This time he took with him a spade and not an axe.
Together they carefully dug up three trees - one for each of
the children; a tiny tree, a middle size tree and one a bit bigger.

Back home they planted the biggest tree in the garden, the middle size one near the house, and the tiny tree in a pot near the door.

So when next Christmas came they would have fir trees that would keep growing, and not have to be thrown out and burned like the poor Little Fir Tree!

As the years went by, the children decorated their trees every Christmas. On the two outside, they tied hundreds of glistening lamps. The smallest tree was carried inside every year until it grew too big for the house.

Now the children have grown up and have children of their own - and grandchildren. The three fir trees have grown, and now they are the tallest in the valley. And every Christmas Eve, they shine so brightly, for all the world to see.

THE NUTCRACKER

Re-told by Anne McKie. Illustrated by Ken McKie.

This enchanting tale took place
almost a century ago. It is a story full
of fantasy and perhaps a little magic.
You may think it was all just a dream
or did it really happen?

Every Christmas Eve, Mayor Stahlbaum
gave a grand party for his son and
daughter and all their young friends.

Now Mayor Stahlbaum was a very rich man, and young Fritz and Clara had a huge nursery full of expensive and unusual toys.

Clara had so many different dolls - she couldn't remember all their names. While her brother Fritz had too many soldiers to count! These soldiers were kept in a model fort twice as high as Fritz himself!

At last it was Christmas Eve and the party was in full swing. Clara and Fritz and their young guests eagerly unwrapped the presents that lay beneath the sparkling Christmas tree.

What fun it was. The children joined in all the games and dancing. They made so much noise the grown-ups felt quite tired out.

It was on that night that a very strange guest arrived at the party. It was Herr Drosselmeyer, Clara's godfather. He was a rather odd old gentleman who made fantastic toys, so life-like, the children were almost afraid to touch them.

Clara and Fritz were never quite sure if they were real or not.

This Christmas Eve, the old man had brought a very special present for Clara. It was a Nutcracker doll in the shape of a soldier.

"This is my favourite Christmas present of all!" cried Clara with delight. "Isn't my Nutcracker handsome?" and she held up her doll for all to see.

"I think he's the ugliest thing I ever saw!" shouted Clara's brother. It was getting late and young Fritz was tired (and had eaten far too many sweets.)

"Give it to me!" he whined. Quick as a flash Fritz grabbed the Nutcracker, pushed a huge hazelnut into its mouth and jammed it shut.

There was a loud crack and the doll's head was split. The nut rolled out and Fritz flung the Nutcracker onto the floor in temper.

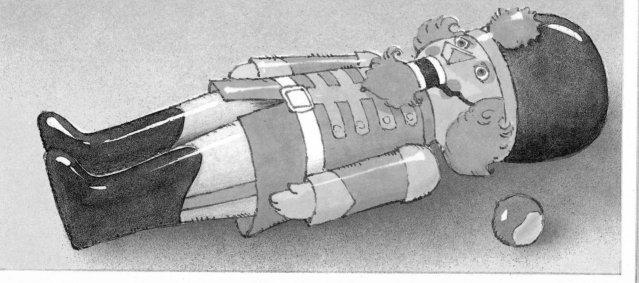

Near to tears, Clara picked up her broken Nutcracker. But Herr Drosselmeyer gently tied his handkerchief round the doll's head and whispered, "In the morning it will be handsome once more!"

Late that night, when all the house was asleep, Clara crept down to the nursery.

As the clock struck midnight, Clara glanced up and was very startled to see Herr Drosselmeyer sitting right on the very top.

What a fright Clara got. Far across the floor, from every corner of her nursery, swarms of mice came scampering towards her!

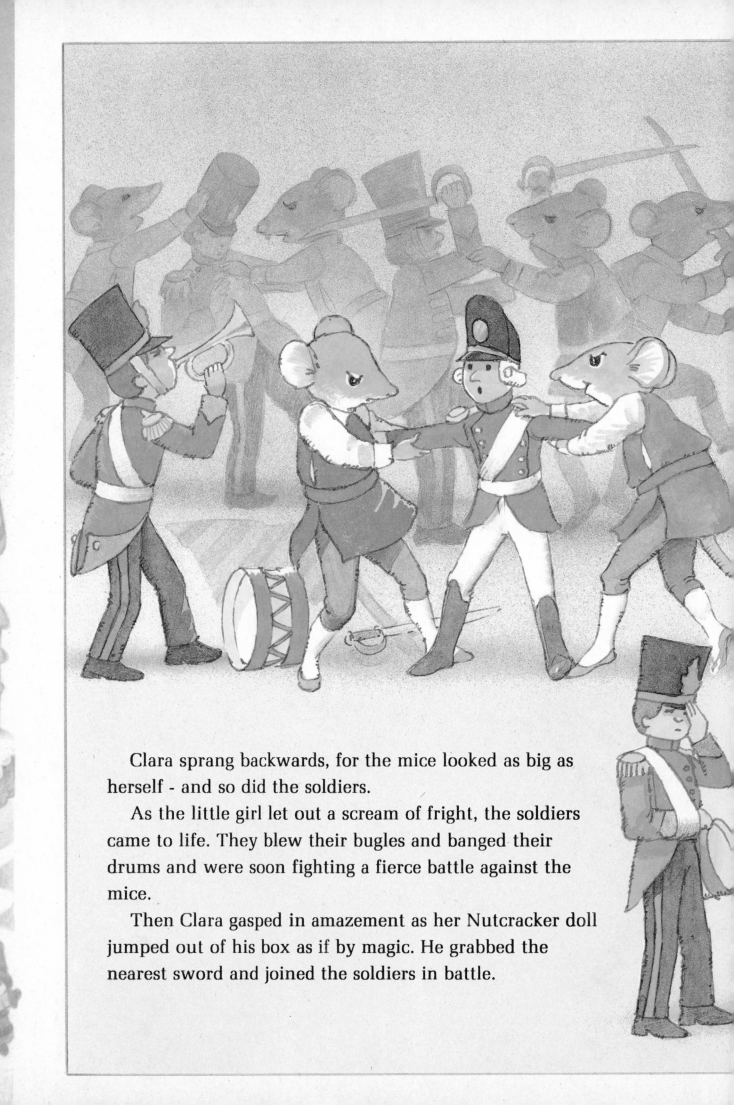

Clara sprang backwards, for the mice looked as big as herself - and so did the soldiers.

As the little girl let out a scream of fright, the soldiers came to life. They blew their bugles and banged their drums and were soon fighting a fierce battle against the mice.

Then Clara gasped in amazement as her Nutcracker doll jumped out of his box as if by magic. He grabbed the nearest sword and joined the soldiers in battle.

All of a sudden from the depth of the army of mice, sprang the evil Mouse King. He had a golden crown on his head and was waving a great sharp sword.

It was quite clear that the mice were winning. There were so many of them.

As the Mouse King came towards the Nutcracker with his sharp sword, Clara pulled off her shoe and aimed it at his head. The shoe caught the Mouse King off guard and he fell to the ground.

In a trice, all the mice vanished, and standing in the Nutcracker's place - was a handsome prince!

"Come with me, Clara!" said the Nutcracker Prince, "and I will take you to a wonderful land!"

Without another word, he whisked Clara off through the wondrous Kingdom of Snow, where the little snowflakes danced in and out of the glittering trees.

The Nutcracker Prince had Clara by the hand and soon they came to the marvellous Land of Sweets, and there at the palace to greet them was the Sugar Plum Fairy.

"Clara saved me from the wicked Mouse King!" the Prince smiled as he told the Fairy about their battle with the mice.

"You must be a very brave girl!" the Sugar Plum Fairy told Clara. "Sit here in the place of honour and receive our grateful thanks."

With that she led Clara to a marzipan throne next to the Prince, clapped her hands and cried, "Let the celebrations begin!"

First came dancers from Spain and from Arabia - Clara was enchanted.

Next came acrobats from China and swirling, stamping Cossacks from Russia - Clara was spellbound.

Last of all came the twirling, whirling Flower Dolls that waltzed with the Sugar Plum Fairy - Clara was lost in a world of fantasy.

Then everyone in the Land of Sweets began to wave goodbye, and Clara felt herself floating on a big soft cloud, just like a dream.

Very gently she drifted far away until the Sugar Plum Fairy and the Nutcracker Prince slowly faded, and the magical Land of Sweets was left far behind.

The next thing Clara knew, she was lying on the nursery floor back in her own house, and held tightly in her arms was her Nutcracker doll.

The little girl realised it was morning. Had it all been just a lovely dream?

Clara ran to the nursery window. As she looked out that cold Christmas Day, she could just make out the dark figure of Herr Drosselmeyer disappearing down the street in the softly falling snow...